# THE GREAT FAIRY TALE DISASTER

HODDER CHILDREN'S BOOKS

First published in Great Britain in 2012 by
Hodder Children's Books
This edition published in 2015 by
Hodder and Stoughton

1 3 5 7 9 10 8 6 4 2

Text copyright © David Conway, 2012
Illustrations copyright © Melanie Williamson, 2012

A CIP catalogue record for this book
is available from the British Library.

ISBN 978 0 340 99643 0

Printed and bound in China

Hodder Children's Books
An imprint of
Hachette Children's Group
Part of Hodder and
Stoughton
Carmelite House
50 Victoria Embankment
London EC4Y 0DZ

An Hachette UK Company
www.hachette.co.uk

www.hachettechildrens.co.uk

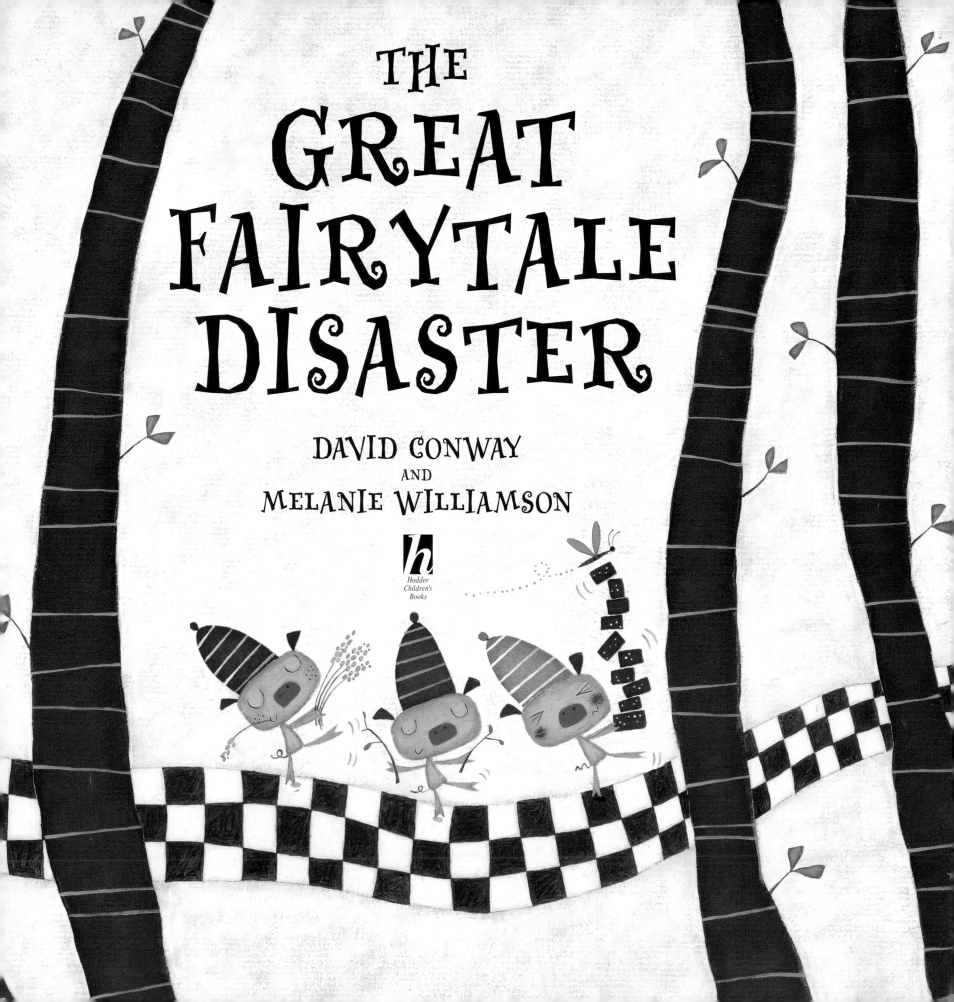

# THE
# GREAT
# FAIRYTALE
# DISASTER

## DAVID CONWAY
### AND
## MELANIE WILLIAMSON

Hodder
Children's
Books

# ONCE UPON A TIME there lived
an old Big Bad Wolf. He no longer had any huff and puff to blow
down the Three Little Pigs' houses and he'd had
enough of falling into hot water.

"What I need," the wolf thought to himself, "is a nice **relaxing** fairy tale for a change." So he scampered off into the pages of The Fairy Tale Book to find one.

**Cinderella** was busy sweeping and hadn't noticed the wolf's dark shadow appear in the doorway.

"I want to be in your tale!" he growled.
"Of c-oo-u-rr-se," stammered a frightened Cinderella.
"Take my place!"

Just then, the fairy godmother arrived.

"I know you'd love to go to the ball," she said to the wolf. "And so you shall!" There was a flick of a wand and a burst of light...

"Wolves don't wear dresses!" cried the wolf, hobbling off in glass slippers to find a different tale.

Soon after, the Big Bad Wolf crept up behind Jack on the **magic beanstalk**. Jack trembled as he let the wolf into his fairy tale...

The Big Bad Wolf was climbing up the beanstalk

when he saw two HUGE feet and heard a

horrible giant voice bawling:

"FEE, FIE, FO, FUM!"

"This tale's too scary!"

cried the wolf as he

slid back down

the beanstalk

to find another one.

Then the Big Bad Wolf found Sleeping Beauty snoring softly in her bed. "WAKEY! WAKEY!" he snarled. "Out you get!"

There the Big Bad Wolf lay, so beautiful that the prince could not turn his eyes away. He knelt down and gave the wolf a kiss...

"YUCK!" spluttered the Big Bad Wolf, "I HATE being kissed!" So he dashed away to try his luck elsewhere.

The Big Bad Wolf ran to the Three Bears' empty cottage in the forest. He opened the door and stepped into the tale. "Yum!" he said. "Porridge! My favourite."

The big bowl of porridge was too **hot**.

The second bowl was too **cold**.

But the littlest bowl was just right, so the wolf ate it **all up!**

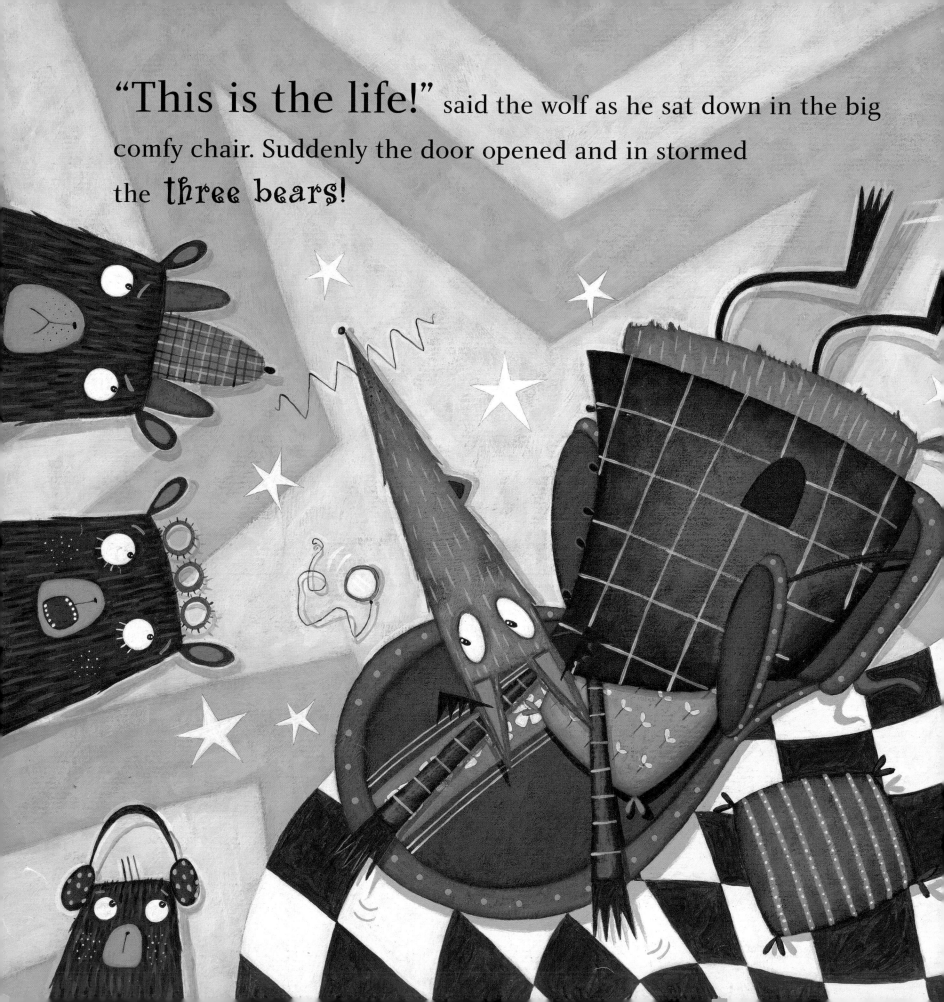

"This is the life!" said the wolf as he sat down in the big comfy chair. Suddenly the door opened and in stormed the three bears!

"Where's Goldilocks?" demanded Daddy Bear.

"What are you doing in our fairy tale?" scowled Mummy Bear.

"And where's my porridge?" cried Baby Bear.

The wolf made a dash for it, but the three bears chased
after him into the next fairy tale...

And then the next...

"Who's that tripping over my bridge!" roared the troll.

"I'll eat you for breakfast."

And before you could say, "Mirror, mirror, on the wall, who is fairest of all?" there was chaos and confusion everywhere!

The princess didn't kiss a frog but she did kiss a Billy Goat Gruff

Hansel and Gretel
pushed Prince Charming
into an oven.

And **Puss in Boots** pricked his
paw on a spindle and fell asleep
for a hundred years.

"What a mess!" cried the Big Bad Wolf and he escaped back through the pages of the book to the Three Little Pigs...

"Little pigs! Little pigs! Let me come in!" huffed the Big Bad Wolf. "No, not by the hair of our chinny chin chins," said the little pigs. "We will **NOT** let you in."

But the wolf had already clambered up onto the roof and he was coming down the chimney...

...only to land SPLASH in a pot
of hot water!

"Oooh, not again!" cried the wolf.

And that was the end
of the fairy tale troubles.

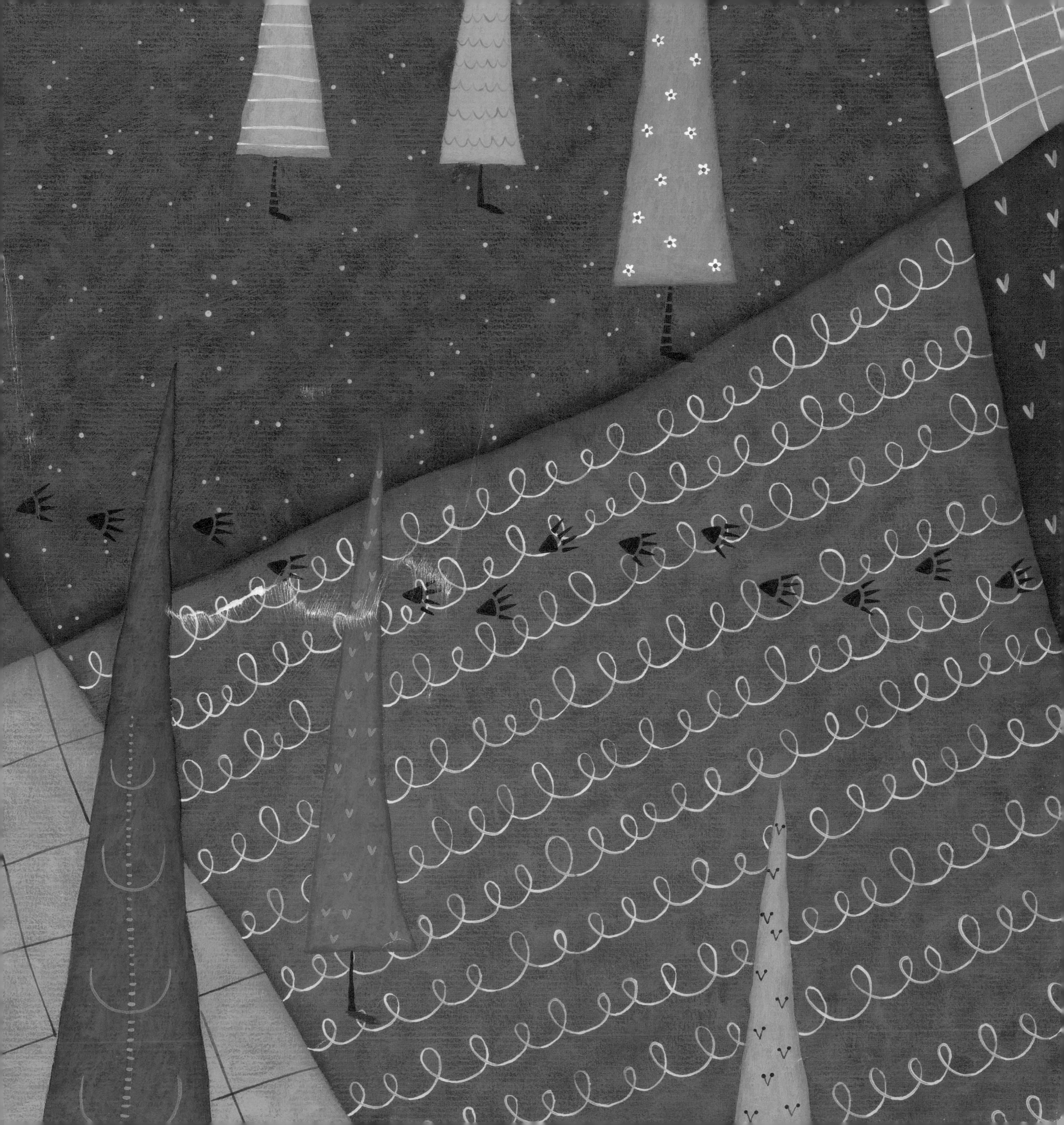

BOOKS BY DAVID CONWAY AND MELANIE WILLIAMSON:

THE GREAT NURSERY RHYME DISASTER
DAVID CONWAY
978 0 340 94508 7

DAVID CONWAY AND MELANIE WILLIAMSON
THE GREAT FAIRY TALE DISASTER
With the Best-Loved Fairy Tales
978 0 340 99643 0